In memory of Rachel Held Evans.
The world is better because of
your love, life, and words.

Text copyright © 2020 by Matthew Paul Turner
Cover art and interior illustrations copyright © 2020 by Gillian Gamble

Published in the United States by Convergent Books, an imprint of Random House, a division of Penguin Random House LLC, New York.
convergentbooks.com

Convergent Books is a registered trademark, and its C colophon is a trademark of Penguin Random House LLC.

Library of Congress Cataloging-in-Publication Data is available upon request.

ISBN 978-0-525-65066-9
eBook ISBN 978-0-525-65069-0

Printed in the United States of America

Cover design by Mark D. Ford

10 9 8 7 6 5 4 3 2 1

WHEN GOD MADE THE WORLD

Matthew Paul Turner   illustrated by Gillian Gamble

CONVERGENT

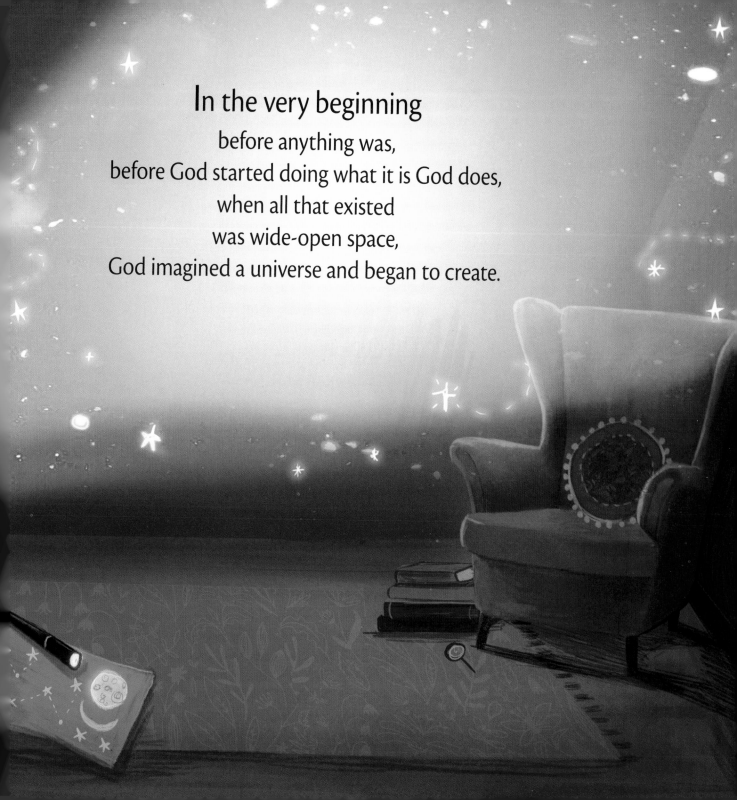

In the very beginning

before anything was,
before God started doing what it is God does,
when all that existed
was wide-open space,
God imagined a universe and began to create.

God hung trillions of lights,
stars big and stars bright.
God turned the dark sky into a glorious sight.

God put planets in places,
with moons in some cases,
and galaxies that reach the outermost spaces.

God made comets that fly
with tails through the sky
and asteroids and meteors that sometimes zoom by.

And with cosmic explosions,
God set space in motion,
causing planets to orbit their suns with devotion.

And somewhere amid all the swirling light,
inside a cluster of milky white,
among stars and planets and cosmic dust,
God made a place for the story of us.

'Cause when God made the world,
God displayed heaven's glory
for you and for me and for all the world's stories.

Our planet God made a blue and green sphere
and designed it to orbit the sun once a year.

God made daytime and nighttime, climates and seasons,
and all kinds of weather that varies by region.

God made continents and oceans, islands and seas,
a north and south pole that God put in deep freeze.

God carved rivers and brooks,
mountains and caves,
made beaches with sand
and huge crashing waves.

God made tropics and plateaus,
glaciers and meadows,
marshes and tundras,
and erupting volcanoes.

God made some places high,
with peaks in the sky,
and places where snowflakes
still fall in July.

And in quite a few spots, God made it so hot,
should you visit, just know that you must drink a lot.

God made valleys so low and geysers that blow.
And under Earth's surface, God put wellsprings that flow.

Then, with gardens and forests and other things green,
God made Earth come to life, using soil and seed.

God made cypress and pines, bushes and vines,
all kinds of trees with leaves God designed.

Plants full of flavor, like basil and thyme,
and trees that grow citrus, like grapefruit and lime.

God made flowering plants and plants that enchant.
While most you can touch, God made some that you can't.

Roses—be warned!—are prickly with thorns,
and there's an African melon God covered in horns.

And poison ivy's backlash? Giving you a rash!
Wherever it touches, you'll itch and you'll scratch.

But don't let that stop you...

Run barefoot through grass,
pick a flower or two or a bouquet, perhaps.

Find a tree you can climb, or with a seat and some twine,
build your very own swing or a backyard zip line.

And when you eat grapes
or pour syrup on crepes

or into a forest you go to escape,
give thanks to God for all that God made,
for the fruit and the syrup, for the trees and the shade.

'Cause when God made the world,
God did all that God could
to create every detail for our joy and our good.

Now, what happened next is a mystery at best,
but God made a bird, and that bird made a nest.

So God filled the sky, perhaps over time,
with birds and more birds, and most learned how to fly.

God made bluebirds and blackbirds,
big birds and small birds,
a few birds quite absurd,
and the loudest birds you've ever heard.

Crows crowed, doves cooed,
chickens clucked, owls hooed,
robins chirped, pheasants whirred.
The world got noisy when God made birds.

Then, the oceans God filled
with fish, sharks, and krill,
creatures God made with fins and with gills.

Swordfish and trout,
fish sleek and fish stout,
and whales that God made to breathe through a spout.

God made sea rays and eels,
fish red, yellow, or teal,
and some fish so odd that they hardly look real.
Like a fish that has fangs or a monster-like face,
or a fish that flies or makes its body inflate.

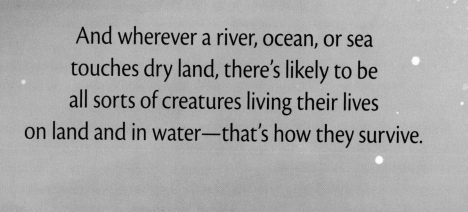

And wherever a river, ocean, or sea
touches dry land, there's likely to be
all sorts of creatures living their lives
on land and in water—that's how they survive.

Like otters and frogs, turtles on logs,
and crocodiles gathering in swampy bogs.

And then God made cows, horses, and goats,
and God made gibbons with inflatable throats.

God planned lions to roar and tigers to pounce,
and kangaroos, God thought, *Let's make you bounce.*

God made bears to growl, moles to plow,
and, under full moons, coyotes to howl.

Donkeys brayed,
giraffes bleated,
jaguars preyed,
rhinos stampeded . . .

bunnies hopped,
beavers chopped,
and, in muddy pools, hippos plopped.

Yes, all living creatures from whales to snails,
from those covered with feathers to those covered with scales,
each God designed with a home in mind,
to develop and evolve if needed over time.

'Cause when God made the world, every creature on Earth
became a part of life's circle, having value and worth.

And God made people,
people like you and me.

People with souls, people with stories,
a global family tree.

God made us all flesh and bone, covered in skin,
and made all our bodies to have hearts beating within.

God gave us bellies and legs, fingers and toes,
and fashioned our faces with eyes, mouth, and a nose.

God made our bodies uniquely equipped
for walking and talking, to eat and to skip.

God wired our brains to feel love and feel pain,
to process and learn, to read and retain.

But despite all we share, we're also unique.
God made us all human, with just a few tweaks.

Each of our faces, bodies, and traits,
our skin tones, our features—God did create.

God made some people shy and some people loud
and some who thrive in the midst of a crowd.

Some make music, and some like math,
and some are prone to blaze their own path.

But always remember, 'cause this much is true,
God had a purpose for making you **YOU**.

So use every gift, every talent or shtick.
Make the world better with your God-given trick.

Bring smiles to faces, show love and good graces
to those who need hope in all different places.

Discover a star, a planet, or moon,
or help keep a forest from dying too soon.

Save a whale, hug a tree, protect every bee.
Recycle, repurpose, reject apathy.

'Cause all of creation whispers God's story—
the mountain, the ocean, the blue morning glory,
the raindrops, the sunshine,
the grapes on the grapevine.
With nature, God gives us a glimpse of divine.

And just like a star might showcase God's light
or a waterfall give us a sign of God's might,
the same could be said of me and of you—
how we live, how we love, tells God's story too.

'Cause when God made the world
and the world started spinning,
the story God wrote was just a beginning.